a meal of the stars

poems

up

and

down

by

Dana

Jensen

illustrated

by

Tricia

Tusa

HOUGHTON MIFFLIN BOOKS FOR CHILDREN

Houghton Mifflin Harcourt

Boston New York 2012

Houghton Mifflin Books for Children is an imprint of
Houghton Mifflin Harcourt Publishing Company.

www.hmhbooks.com

The text of this book is set in TuffHalo.
The illustrations are watercolor and ink.

Library of Congress Cataloging-in-Publication Data
Jensen, Dana.
A meal of the stars : poems up and down / by Dana
Jensen ; illustrated by Tricia Tusa.
p. cm.
ISBN 978-0-547-39007-9
I. Tusa, Tricia, ill. II. Title.
PS3610.E5628M43 2012
811'.6—dc22
2011012250

Manufactured in Singapore
TWP 10 9 8 7 6 5 4 3 2 1
4500335513

To Leela —

welcome to the world of books!

—D.J.

For Amelia and Muffin.

—T.T.

stars
the
of
meal
a
make
could
giraffe
the
if
wonder
I
that
as
long
as
neck
a
with

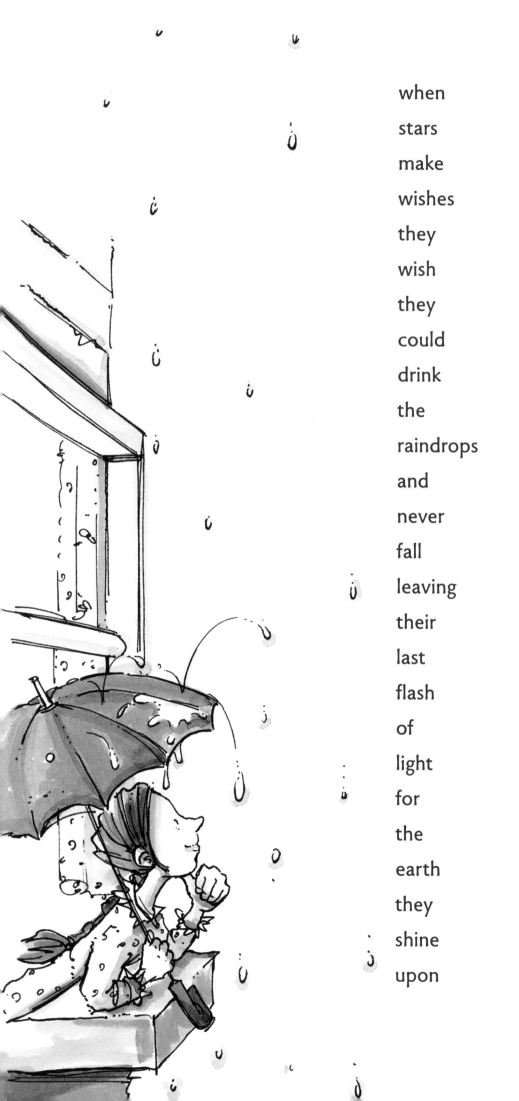

when
stars
make
wishes
they
wish
they
could
drink
the
raindrops
and
never
fall
leaving
their
last
flash
of
light
for
the
earth
they
shine
upon

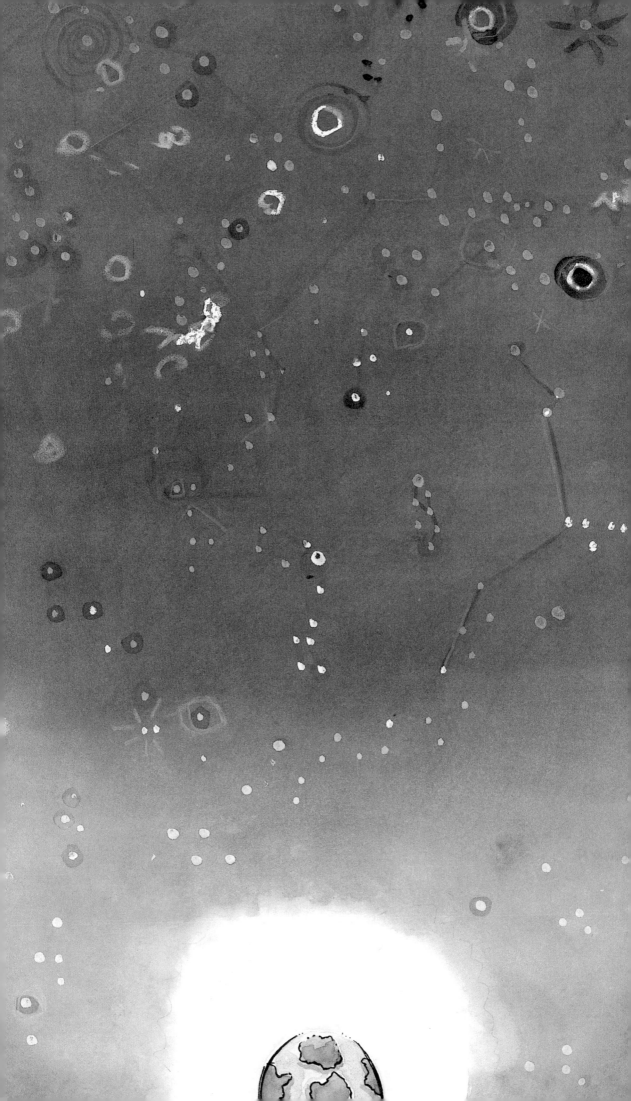

pop!

balloo-
blue
bright
big
a
to
up
rising
string
of
length
the
hand
my
in
gripped
there!

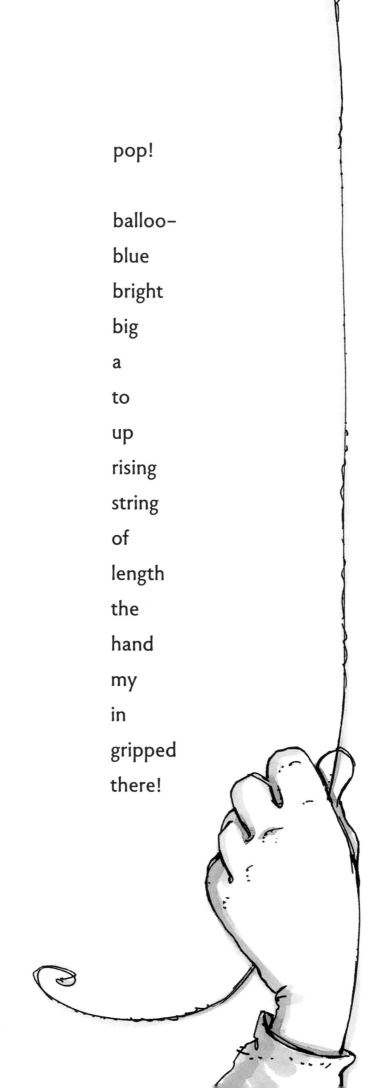

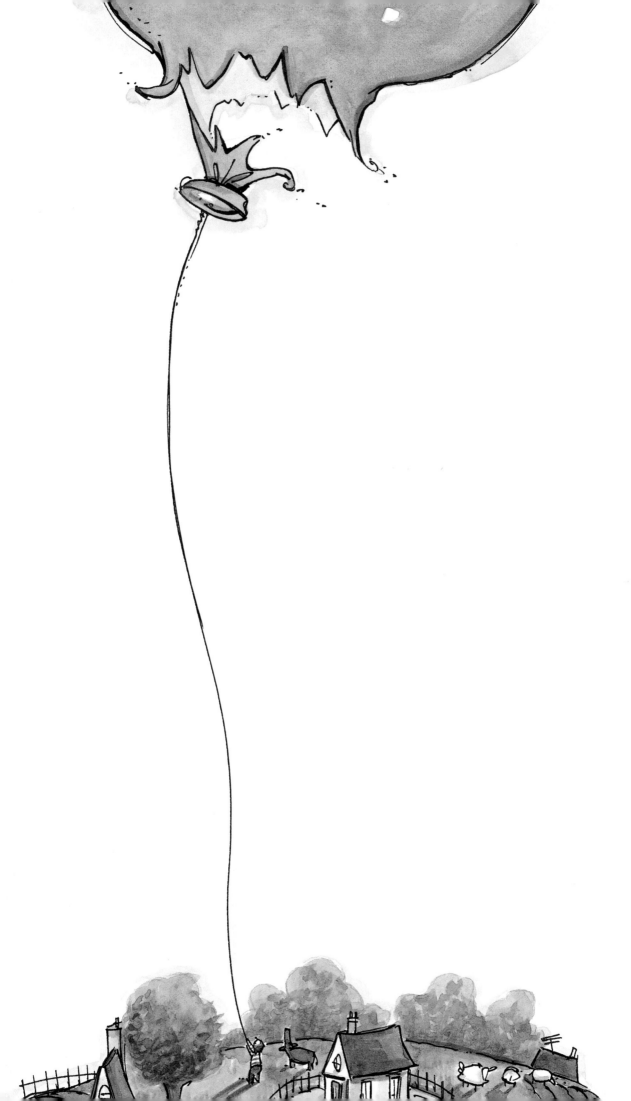

dandelion

swaying

the

of

bed

yellow

the

on

rest

to

climbs

ladybug

the

stem

narrow

long

the

up

as
the
Ferris
wheel
stops
at
its
highest
point
we
gaze
down
upon
the
moving
sounds
and
colors
of
this
carnival
world

is

grandfather

my

than

taller

even

is

it

that

tall

so

is

clock

grandfather

grandfather's

my

space
silent
endless
of
beauty
black
pitch-
the
toward
sky
cerulean
the
across
blasts
rocket
the
smoke
and
fury
and
fire
with

the
bongs
of
far-
off
bells
float
down
to
us
they
touch
us
with
their
songs
they
walk
with
us
a
spell

up
time
first
the
missed
he
spot
the
paint
to
house
the
of
peak
highest
the
to
ladder
the
climbs
dad
my
rung
by
rung

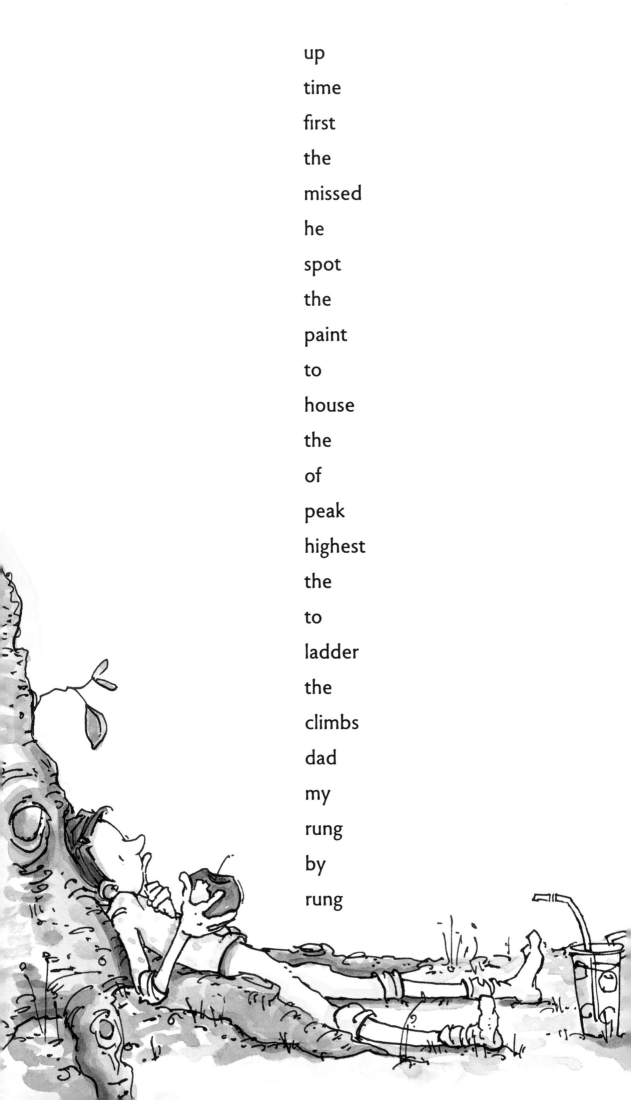

me
except
left
is
one
no
until
off
get
people
the
floor
by
floor
and
up
slowly
goes
elevator
the
up
up

roaring
crashing
sparkling
and
white
oh
what
a
thunder
heaving
its
mighty
heart
the
waterfall
splashes
out
its
lovely
blue
music
on
the
slippery
rocks
below

away
far
skies
blue
in
clouds
and
birds
with
dance
and
loop
to
trees
leafing
above
soar
will
spring
in
kite
paper
a
tight
is
string
and
right
is
wind
if

me
tickle
and
in
sneak
don't
snowflakes
the
that
so
says
always
mom
my
chin
my
to
up
way
the
all
zip

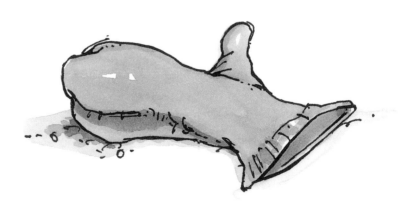

again
hatch
to
songs
and
birds
and
eggs
and
spring
for
wait
can't
boughs
tree
highest
the
in
nest
the
long
winter
all

from
the
top
of
my
head
to
the
tips
of
my
toes
no
one
is
standing
here
except
me